Investigate Science

Animals All Around

by Melissa Stewart

Content Adviser: Jan Jenner, Ph.D.

Reading Adviser: Rosemary G. Palmer, Ph.D.,
Department of Literacy, College of Education,
Boise State University

COMPASS POINT BOOKS MINNEAPOLIS, MINNESOTA

Compass Point Books
3109 West 50th St., #115
Minneapolis, MN 55410

Visit Compass Point Books on the Internet at *www.compasspointbooks.com* or e-mail your request to *custserv@compasspointbooks.com*

Photographs ©: Jose Luis Pelaez, Inc./Corbis, cover (middle); Photo Network/Mark Newman, cover, 1; PhotoDisc, 4 (right), 29 (middle right); Index Stock Imagery, 4 (top left), 9; Image Source, 4 (middle left), 29 (top left & top right); Stockbyte, 4 (bottom left), 21; Gregg Andersen, 5, 10, 11 (all), 15, 24; Robert McCaw, 6, 19, 22, 23, 25 (bottom); Tom Stewart/Corbis, 7, 18; DigitalVision, 8, 13, 29 (middle left & bottom left); Unicorn Stock Photos/ Martha McBride, 12; Dwight R. Kuhn, 14, 16; Corel, 17; Rob & Ann Simpson, 20; Randall B. Henne/Dembinsky Photo Associates, 25 (top); Hans Reinhard/Bruce Coleman Inc., 29 (bottom right).

Editor: Christianne C. Jones
Photo Researcher: Svetlana Zhurkina
Designer: The Design Lab
Illustrator: Jeffrey Scherer

Library of Congress Cataloging-in-Publication Data
Stewart, Melissa.
Animals all around / by Melissa Stewart.
    p. cm. — (Investigate science)
Summary: Introduces common animals in everyday surroundings, their life cycles, and body parts.
ISBN 0-7565-0594-1 (hardcover)
1. Animals—Juvenile literature. 2. Nature study—Juvenile literature. [1. Animals. 2. Nature study.] I. Title.
    II. Series.
QL49.S763 2004
590—dc22   2003018843

Note to Readers: To learn about animals, scientists observe them closely. They draw and write about everything they see. Later, they use their drawings and notes to help them remember exactly what they observed.

This book will help you study animals like a scientist. To get started, you will need to get a notebook and a pencil.

As you read the book, be sure to stop and do each activity. Remember that animals are living things and can feel things just like you. Treat them gently and do not take them out of their natural environment.

In the Doing More section in the back of the book, you will find step-by-step instructions for more fun science experiments and activities.

In this book, words that are defined in the glossary are in **bold** the first time they appear in the text.

Table of Contents

As you read this book, be on the lookout for these special symbols:

Read directions *very carefully.*

Ask an adult for help.

Turn to the Doing More section in the back of the book.

Your backyard is
a great place to
look for animals!

4

Animals Are Everywhere

Go outside and look around. How many different kinds of animals do you see? Dogs, cats, and squirrels are animals. Birds, butterflies, and earthworms are animals, too. Animals come in many shapes, colors, and sizes. They live in many different places and eat all kinds of foods.

Grab a notebook and pencil. Make a list of all the animals you see in your backyard or at a nearby park. Draw pictures of three or more of the animals you see. Can you think of anything that all these animals have in common?

More than 700 kinds of birds live in North America. To see some of them up close, have an adult help you set up a bird feeder outside one of the windows of your home.

Observe how the birds behave. Notice how they fly. Watch what they eat and how they eat. Do different birds eat different kinds of birdseed?

Now go outside, and sit quietly near the bird feeder. When some birds are at the feeder, stand up slowly and walk toward them. How close can you get before the birds fly away? Try this several times. Do some birds fly away sooner than others? How do the birds know you are coming? Write down your observations in your notebook.

Setting up your own bird feeder is a great way to attract birds.

The color of a frog's skin helps it blend into its surroundings and hide from predators.

All animals need to find food and stay away from **predators.** They keep away from predators in different ways. Most insects fly, fish swim, and dogs run. A frog's dull skin helps it blend in with its surroundings, but a bird's bright feathers make it stand out. The body of each animal is suited for the way it lives.

Now draw a frog, a bird, a fish, a dog, an insect, and an earthworm. Label the most important body parts of each animal. What do all of these animals have in common?

A butterfly can fly away from its predators

Living and Growing

A rock and an egg look very similar on the outside.

Look closely at an egg and a rock. They may look similar on the outside, but their insides are very different.

Eggs are made by animals, and they can grow into new animals. Crack open an egg and look for the yellow yolk inside. If a chick were growing inside the egg, it would eat the yolk.

Now try to break a rock in half. It's not so easy. A rock is hard and solid. The inside looks just like the outside. Rocks form as mountains break down. They are not made by living things, so they cannot develop into new creatures.

You don't need to use a lot of force to crack open an egg.

Compare the insides of the rock and the egg.

11

You can look at eggs in a nest, but do not touch them.

Many animals begin life inside an egg, but not all eggs look the same. In the spring, search for bird eggs. You can find nests on the ground or in trees. Look for frog eggs floating on top of ponds. Use a hand lens to spot tiny insect eggs on the bottoms of leaves.

Study these eggs carefully, but do not touch them. If you touch bird eggs, mother birds may abandon their nests. If you touch frog or insect eggs, they may never hatch.

When scientists want to remember what they have observed, they may draw pictures. You can do this, too. Then you can ask questions like a scientist. Why are some eggs larger than others? Why do different animals lay their eggs in different places?

Some birds hide their eggs in a deep nest.

Ladybug eggs are usually found on the leaves or stems of plants.

Think About It!

In the fall or winter, use a hand lens to look for insect eggs on plant stems and leaves. During the spring, observe the insect eggs every day. Before and after they hatch, keep careful records like a scientist. Write down the date, the temperature, and the weather conditions. After the eggs hatch, spend some time observing the young insects. Notice how they move and what they eat. Take notes, and draw pictures of everything you see.

Use a hand lens to get a better view of insect eggs.

Many young insects look similar to their parents, but most animals look quite different. Have an adult help you search for young and adult animals at a local park. Do young birds look like their parents? What about frogs, squirrels, and snakes?

Now have an adult take you to a pet store. Look carefully at the puppies and kittens. Then observe some adult dogs and cats. Pay special attention to the size of the animals' eyes and ears. Look at the length of each animal's tail and legs. Make a list of how the older animals are different from the younger ones.

Young aphids look just like adult aphids except they are much smaller.

Young birds must develop before they look like adult birds.

Many animals sleep during the day and come out at night. If you haven't spent much time outdoors after dark, you might be surprised at how different the world can seem.

 To find out, ask an adult to go outside with you on a summer evening. Be sure to take a notebook, a pencil, and a flashlight. You may also need some bug spray.

Find a safe place and sit quietly. Close your eyes and listen. Make a list of noises that come from human-made things, such as car engines or sirens. Make a different list of natural sounds, such as the wind or crickets. How many animal sounds can you identify?

Return to the same spot the next morning. Do you hear the same noises? Make a list of noises you hear only during the day. Compare your three lists. What's different about each list?

If you listen closely, you may even hear an owl at night!

19

Deer have a harder time finding food in the winter because their surroundings change.

Scientists often repeat their experiments to see if they get the same results. You can, too. Keep track of noises you hear in the same spot on a winter night. Are there any differences from the noises you heard in the summer?

You will probably hear fewer animal sounds in the winter. That's because winter is a difficult time for animals. They have trouble staying warm and finding food.

Animals have different ways of surviving. Many animals travel to warmer places in the winter. They can find plenty of food and stay warm. Some animals hibernate in the winter. They store up food and sleep through the winter. They become active again in the spring.

Most birds travel to warmer places for the winter.

Animal Signs

Have you ever seen a raccoon or a fox? Some animals are hard to spot. However, you can still find signs that tell you where animals have been.

The next time you're in a field or forest, look for bird feathers, bits of fur, claw marks, old snake skins, **animal tracks,** and other **animal** **signs.** Collect some and take them home. Ask an adult to help you identify the animal that left each sign.

A bear left claw marks on this tree.

23

Look for insects and animals in their natural environment.

If you look carefully, you can also discover where different kinds of animals live. An animal's home protects it from predators and the weather. Draw pictures of birds, ants, and beavers, and their homes.

Now that you've spent some time observing animals, you have a better understanding of how they live and how they change as they grow. The next time you're in a natural area, pay close attention. There are animals all around.

Ants may build their homes on your driveway or sidewalk.

Beavers build their homes in the water.

25

Activity One

On page 6 you learned that a bird feeder is a good place to watch birds in your own backyard. If you'd like to watch birds without them knowing it, try making a bird blind. A bird blind will allow you to watch the birds without them seeing you. Ask an adult for help with each of the following steps.

1. Find a large piece of cardboard or a cardboard box about the same size as the windows in your home. If you use a box, cut off the flaps and one side.

2. Hold the cardboard up to the window. Use a pencil and ruler to mark where an adult should cut two eye slits for you to see through.

3. Use strong tape to mount your bird blind to the window near the bird feeder. Birds won't know when you are watching them, so you can observe their natural behavior.

Activity Two

On page 19 you learned about animals that only come out at night. If you'd like to see some common nighttime insects, try this experiment.

1. Borrow an old white T-shirt from an adult. Tape it to the wall below a porch light.

2. Sit very still and wait for insects to come. As soon as an insect lands on the T-shirt, look at it closely and then draw it. Try to stay still so you don't scare the insect away.

3. Ask an adult to help you use a field guide to identify the insects.

4. Try the same experiment at different times of the year. When do the most insects land on the T-shirt? Why?

Activity Three

On page 22 you learned that animal signs can help you find out what animals live in an area. When the ground is muddy or covered with snow, some of the easiest animal signs to spot are animal tracks. To see animal tracks any time of the year, try this experiment.

1. Find a quiet spot in your yard. Put a large metal tray, such as a cookie sheet, on the ground and cover it with a thin layer of flour.

2. Place a small spoonful of peanut butter in the middle of the tray and leave.

3. Return a few hours later. If the peanut butter is gone, whatever ate it will have left behind a trail of footprints. Look at the common animal footprints shown on the next page. Do any of them match?

4. To find other kinds of prints, try this experiment in different places. Go back to the spot during different times of the day. You can also try using other types of bait.

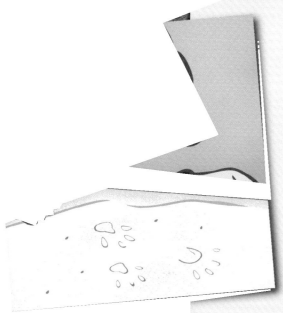

Cat

Dog

Chipmunk

Bird

Mouse

Squirrel

Animal Tracks

Did any of these animals leave the tracks on your metal tray? If not, ask an adult to help you use a field guide to identify the animal that made the prints.

Glossary

abandon to leave alone

animal sign something left behind by an animal

animal tracks a trail of footprints made in mud or snow

hand lens a tool that makes objects look bigger than they really are; sometimes called a magnifying glass

hibernate to be inactive or to sleep through winter

observe to use all five senses to gather information about the world

predators animals that hunt other animals for food

survive to stay safe and alive

To Find Out More

At the Library

Fraser, Mary Ann. *Where Are the Night Animals?* New York:
HarperCollins, 1999.

Hewitt, Sally. *Animal Homes.* Chicago: World Book, 1999.

Hewitt, Sally. *All Kinds of Animals.* New York: Children's Press, 1998.

Dendy, Leslie. *Animal Tracks, Scats, and Signs.* Minneapolis:
Northword Press, 1998.

Places to Visit

Smithsonian National Zoological Park

3001 Connecticut Ave. N.W.

Washington, DC 20008

See more than 2,700 interesting animals from all over the world.

On the Web

For more information on **animals**, use FactHound to track down
Web sites related to this book.

1. Go to *www.compasspointbooks.com/facthound*

2. Type in this book ID: 0756505941

3. Click on the *Fetch It* button.

Your trusty FactHound will fetch the best Web sites for you!

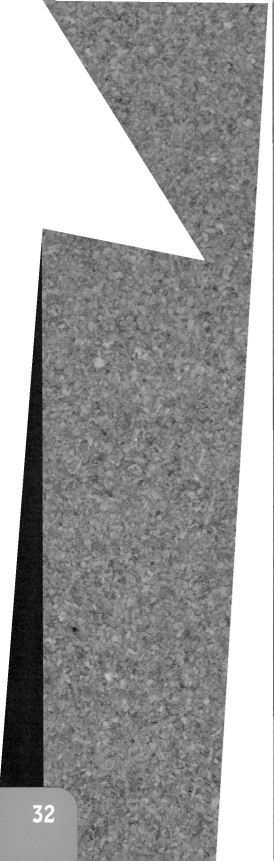

Index

About the Author

Melissa Stewart earned a bachelor's degree in biology from Union College and a master's degree in science and environmental journalism from New York University. After editing children's science books for nearly a decade, she decided to become a full-time writer. She has written more than 50 science books for children and contributed articles to ChemMatters, Instructor, MATH, National Geographic World, Natural New England, Odyssey, Science World, and Wild Outdoor World. She also teaches writing workshops and develops hands-on science programs for schools near her home in Northborough, Massachusetts.